ISBN 1-58987-007-7

Published in 2003 by Kindermusik International, Inc.

Do-Re-Me & You! is a trademark of Kindermusik International, Inc.

Printed in China
First Printing, July 2003

Noodles
from
Scratch

by Harold P. Gershenson

illustrated by Christopher Mills

Sylvia Sheep was ready to munch;
It seemed like hours since she'd seen her lunch.
But she did not want veggies, nor bacon, nor cheese.
She did not want kumquats. Nothing would please.

"I want a good supper, but what's there to eat?
I want something tasty, delicious, a treat;
Something *gourmet*ish, filling yet light;
Something most stylish. What would be right?"

3

4

Sylvia pulled out some eggs, a big bowl, and a spoon,
Then a large sack of flour—while humming a tune.
And as she was humming, a plan she did hatch;
"I know what I'm cooking. I'll make noodles from scratch!"

5

And she sang . . .

"Noodles from scratch,
Noodles from scratch,
I'll make a big batch
Of noodles from scratch!"

She picked up the flour and was ready to pour
When Petra the Pelican peeked in through the door.
"Petra, my dear, just in time, what a treasure—
Your beak is just perfect. It will serve for a measure!"

7

"Noodles from scratch,
Noodles from scratch,
We'll make a big batch
Of noodles from scratch!"

When Kevin the Crocodile crawled into the room,
Sylvia caressed him and fell into a swoon.
"Kevin! How clever! I know you've the knack
To help with the eggs. I've a dozen to crack."

9

"Noodles from scratch,
Noodles from scratch,
We'll make a big batch
Of noodles from scratch!"

While they stirred up their dough into a big mess,
Hilda Hippo arrived in her polka-dot dress.
"My handsome Ms. Hippo, you work with such speed,
Please help with the dough. We need you to knead!"

"Noodles from scratch,
Noodles from scratch,
We'll make a big batch
Of noodles from scratch!"

"Let's roll out the dough—it's smooth and elastic.
But what can we roll with to make it fantastic?"
"Good golly," squawked Petra, "Attention! Aloha!
Hilda, my sweetheart, please lend us your boa."

"Noodles from scratch,
Noodles from scratch,
We'll make a big batch
Of noodles from scratch!"

They cut splendid noodles. They left them to dry.
Then they boiled them *al dente*, and sat down with a sigh.
But when they were seated, they discovered a catch.
They'd nothing to put on their noodles from scratch.

16

Yet Sylvia found butter, red sauce, and some cheese,
And they each could put on whatever did please.
They slurped them and glurped them and made such a mess
That Hilda the Hippo had stripes on her dress.

But it made no matter as they all sang . . .

"Noodles from scratch,
Noodles from scratch,
We ate a big batch
Of noodles from scratch!"

Noodles from Scratch
(The Song)

Refrain:
Noodles from scratch,
Noodles from scratch,
We'll make a big batch
Of noodles from scratch!

Crack eggs in the flour,
Crack eggs in the flour,
We'll work for an hour
To crack eggs in the flour.

Let's knead the dough,
Let's knead the dough,
Work fast or work slow
When we knead the dough.

We'll eat with a slurp,
We'll eat with a slurp,
We'll just stop to burp
When we eat with a slurp.

Noodles from Scratch
(The Recipe)

You can make your own noodles from scratch. It's easier than pie with one or two helpers.

You will need:

1¼ cups flour
2 eggs
1 teaspoon salt
1 teaspoon cooking oil

Beat the eggs, salt, and oil together in a small bowl.

In the largest mixing bowl you have, arrange the flour like a doughnut with a very big hole. Pour the egg mixture into the center of the doughnut. Stir the eggs around, gradually incorporating the flour, until you have a nice dough. If it's sticky, add a little more flour.

Divide the dough among the helping hands and thump, bump, and mush the dough (knead it) for ten minutes until it is smooth. If it gets sticky, a little more flour won't hurt.

Roll out the dough until it is as thin as noodles, more or less.

Cut the dough into shapes. Rectangles can be pinched in the middle to make bow ties or rolled around a straw sprayed with cooking oil to make macaroni.

Let the noodles dry on a rack for a couple of hours.

Cook the noodles in a great big pot of boiling water for about four or five minutes, depending on their thickness. When they are just *al dente* (cooked through but still firm, not mushy), remove them from the pot and top with plenty of butter, cheese, or red sauce.